A Gathering of Tales
— from a —
Cosmopolitan Family

Written by
WONDERING WANDERING WRITER
Illustrations by CINNAMOM

AuthorHouse™ UK
1663 Liberty Drive
Bloomington, IN 47403 USA
www.authorhouse.co.uk
UK TFN: 0800 0148641 (Toll Free inside the UK)
UK Local: 02036 956322 (+44 20 3695 6322 from outside the UK)

Because of the dynamic nature of the Internet, any web addresses or links contained in this book may have changed since publication and may no longer be valid. The views expressed in this work are solely those of the author and do not necessarily reflect the views of the publisher, and the publisher hereby disclaims any responsibility for them.

This book is printed on acid-free paper.

ISBN: 978-1-6655-8249-0 (sc)
ISBN: 978-1-6655-8248-3 (e)

Print information available on the last page.

Published by AuthorHouse 03/11/2021

authorHOUSE®

FOREWORD

In the children's book "A Gathering of Tales from a Cosmopolitan Family", readers can discover the magic of the Chuk family. There is the Mother Dreamer Panda, the Father Sturdy Tiger and their two daughters Love Ladybug and Purity Elephant. They are all very different, and each has their own personality. The parents are not necessarily the leaders of the family: the children teach the adults too.

In "A Gathering of Tales from a Cosmopolitan Family", you can develop your imagination and your perceptiveness by adding your own illustrations of some of the characters. If you want to share these with the author, she would be delighted to gather and display your works of art in an exciting online and worldwide exhibition!

"A book is a window on the world", as the illustrator said once during the working process. The author hopes you will start to learn stories from different countries and you will continue to look for them! Here you will find stories from the magic of Scotland, to the mystery of Africa, to the wonders of Europe. Travelling through Europe with ERASMUS and the European Voluntary Service the author of this book was able to discover enchanting worlds and people, involving them in her tales.

The author's wish is that this children's book will entertain not just kids but also adults, and refresh their childhood memories about the wonders of the animal kingdom. "A Gathering of Tales from a Cosmopolitan Family" will be the first one of a series. The Chuk family will continue to tell you stories in order to raise a new generation of cosmopolitan citizens. We should go beyond the borders of nations; it would be a great achievement if this book became a first step towards, quoting Wole Soyinka, "the death of nations and the existence of humanity".

There was once a family called Chuk. The father, Sturdy Tiger, was a hard worker. He could fix everything at home, and he loved to dance with his family. The mother, Dreamer Panda, was a bookworm and she liked to tell her daughters many stories. Their lovely daughters were called Love Lady Bug, and the wee Purity Elephant.

Dreamer Panda woke up early every morning to prepare breakfast for all her family and put the toys away. She loved to wake up Love and Purity by saying, 'Good morning,' in many of the languages of the world:

Ututu oma (Igbo)

Bonjour (French)

Buna dimineata (Romanian)

Buongiorno (Italian)

"Ututu oma, buongiorno, good morning, girls! It is time to start another fun day together!,"

Dreamer Panda sweetly said as she entered the bedroom of her lovely daughters.

"You must know that a long time ago I met a very special friend. Her name was Yana, and she was a beautiful mermaid. She is from Armenia, the land of the pink city, Yerevan. It gets its pretty pink hue from the rosy volcanic rock that was used to construct many of the city's buildings.

Yana told me a lot of stories about her grandma. One thing her granny always said in the morning was, "Breakfast is for the king, lunch is for the prince, and dinner is for the peasant." Let's go have our own!"

The Scottish breakfast made by Dreamer Panda included rashers of bacon, mushrooms, tomatoes, and fried eggs—as the normal English ones do, —plus tattie scones, the Aberdeen rowie (a sort of buttery, salty bread), and the Arbroath smokie fish.

Dreamer Panda put breakfast on the table. Love and Purity ate it with a smile because they loved tattie scones!

In reality, this breakfast was not made all morning by Dreamer Panda. There is a secret in Scotland. Are you ready to discover it?! Dreamer Panda went into their courtyard, followed by her kids.

Dreamer Panda threw some pebbles at the picket fence, and magically turned into a rabbit, who started to squeak the following story.

IT'S YOUR TURN!
USING YOUR IMAGINATION DRAW THE RABBIT HERE!
SNAP IT AND SEND IT TO
ihunanyadiocha2018@gmail.com
TO BE INVOLVED IN A FANTASTIC WORLDWIDE EXHIBITION!

There was once a farmhouse called Fern Glen. All the people were scared of him, even though they had never seen him and had no idea what he looked like. A brownie is not a wicked creature: during the night, he helped people finish chores for just a bowl of milk and porridge. The only person who was not scared at all was the wife of the farmer. One night this gentle lady was taken very ill, and everyone was afraid she was going to die. The farmer was greatly distressed – so were the servants and farmhands – for she had been such a good mistress to all of them that they loved her as if she were their mother. Unluckily, they were all young, and none of them knew very much about illness, so everyone agreed that it would be better to send for an old woman who lived about seven miles away, on the other side of the river, and known to be a very skilful nurse. But who was to go? That was the question. It was already midnight and the way to the old woman's house lay straight through the glen. Whoever travelled that road at night ran the risk of meeting the unwelcome brownie. The farmer would have gone, but he dared not leave his wife alone. So the servants stood in groups about the kitchen, each one telling the other that he or she ought to go. None of them offered to go themselves. They didn't know that the cause of all their terror was standing only a yard or two away, listening with an anxious face from behind the kitchen door. He had come up from his hiding place in the glen as he did every night. But he was still inside the farmhouse, and the light was still on. So he had crept in through the back door to try and find out what the matter was. When he learned from the servants' talk the farmer's wife was sick, his heart sank. And when he heard that the silly servants were so taken up with their own fears that they dared not set out to fetch a nurse for her, he became angry. "Dolts!" He muttered to himself, stamping his queer, long feet on the floor. "They speak as if I were ready to take a bite out of them as soon as I met them. If they only knew the bother it gives me to keep out of their way. But if they go on like this, the bonnie lady will surely die. So it seems that I must go and fetch help myself."

So saying, he left the farm with one of the farmer's horses, and started his travel towards the house of the nurse.

The brownie woke up the woman, telling her his errand. "The mistress of Fern Glen is ill", and there is no one to nurse her but a bunch of empty-headed servants. Will you come with me, and quickly, to save her life?"

"But how am I to get there? Have they sent a cart for me?" Asked the old woman anxiously, for she was familiar with the way to the farm and was nervous of meeting the brownie in the glen. "No, they have sent no cart," replied the brownie shortly. "So you must just climb up behind me on the saddle, and hang on tight to my waist, I promise to bring you to Fern Glen safe and sound." The old woman made haste to dress herself and gather her nurse's bag.

Not a word was spoken until they approached the dreaded glen. Then the old woman felt her courage giving way. "Do you think that there will be any chance of meeting the brownie?" she asked tremulously. "I would not run the risk, for folks say that he is a dodgy creature."

Her companion gave a curious laugh. "Keep up your heart, and don't talk nonsense," he said. "I promise you'll see naught uglier this night than the man whom you ride behind."

"Oh, then, I'm safe and sound," replied the old woman, with a sigh of relief. "Although I haven't seen your face, I warrant that you are a good man, from the care you have shown for your mistress at the farm."

During the trip the woman wondered if that funny man was the brownie. Finally, they came to the farmhouse, and the woman went to the bedroom where the farmer's wife was. Before disappearing into the trees, the brownie told the woman that no one has to be afraid of him. She reported the message to the farm's inhabitants. When the farmer's wife was fine, the people of Fern Glen were no longer afraid of him, and they left out a bowl of milk on the doorstep every night.

Purity Elephant and Love Ladybug were fighting, as sisters do. Purity shouted to her mother: "Mom, Love has broken my doll!"

Love answered: "It's not true! I don't like that stupid doll."

"Well, somebody has cut his hair!" Purity crossed her arms and pouted. To calm herself down, Purity took a deep breath and remembered a story Dreamer Panda told them two days ago.

"Love, do you remember Metekú's story? The Eritrean lad."

Love was in the corner of the room, drawing animals. "No, where is Eritrea?"

"Well, Love, Eritrea is a small country on the horn of Africa. Metekú was an orphan with just a small shack and a cow. After a lot of misfortune, he met a princess. While they were chatting and walking, he gathered her into his arms and bent his head to kiss her."

Love was amazed.

"Thank you so much for telling a love story! Dalu! Grazie! Merci! Multumesc! Asante Sana! Dziekuje! Koszonom!"

"Love, Purity, lunch is ready" Dreamer Panda called them. She smiled because, although Purity is the youngest, she loved to tell a lot of stories, and the whole family was happy to listen to her.

Purity Elephant threw some pebbles at the picket fence, and magically she turned into a mouse, who started to squeak the following story.

NOW, IT'S YOUR TURN!
USING YOUR IMAGINATION DRAW THE MOUSE HERE!
SNAP IT AND SEND IT TO
ihunanyadiocha2018@gmail.com
TO BE INVOLVED IN A FANTASTIC WORLDWIDE EXHIBITION!

N ear Loch Ness lived a family with a mother, a father, and a laddie named Nathan. They lived on a farm, eating what they could bring from the earth. The parents had a discussion about the plough that year: the Dad was now too old to use it, and Nathan was too young. So the husband told his wife he would bring home the horse that lived in the sea. His wife argued that it was a sea kelpie, a spirit, and it was impossible for a man to tame it. The husband did not believe her, so he disappeared out of the door, leaving the family alone, and never came home. Although Nathan and his mother searched and called his name the whole night, the only answer they got was the howling of the wind and the crashing of the waves upon the rocks. The following morning the plough rope and his father's woollen plaid washed up on the shore. Sadly, Nathan brought them home to his mother, who sat weeping by the fire. "Now we will surely starve to death," she cried.

"I'll go to the loch," Nathan told her. "And I'll catch some fish."

"There will be no fish in the waters where a kelpie lives," his mother replied.

"I can but try," said Nathan." He went to the loch side and began to fish. He had sat there most of the day, catching nothing, when an old woman came by collecting firewood.

"A pleasant day," Nathan greeted her, "to be happy in the sun's warmth before it ends."

"That it is," the old woman said, "but I am not warm at night when my bones ache with the cold." Now Nathan's father had often told him that no matter how poor you were, there was always someone poorer. So when Nathan saw that the old woman only had a worn shawl to keep her warm, he went to the cottage and brought out his father's woollen plaid for her.

"I do not take without giving in return," said the old woman, and she gave Nathan her worn shawl in exchange. She stared at him as she did, and said, "It can be better to sit upon a plaidie[1] than wrap it round you."

---

[1]   A large blanket made of wool in a tartan pattern.

That day Nathan caught a fish. The next day, as Nathan was fishing, the old woman came by again.

"Another fine day for you to enjoy," said Nathan.

"That it is," the old woman said. "Although if I had bread in my stomach, I would enjoy it more."

"Here, have mine," Nathan handed the old woman the bread his mother had given him for his breakfast.

"I do not take without giving in return," said the old woman. She gave Nathan a lump of salt in a little pouch. "Salt can be used to kill rather than to cure."

Nathan tied the pouch to the waistband of his trousers. And that day he caught two fish.

On the third day when the old woman came by, Nathan was worried.

A fair day," he said to her. "Good for walking and talking."

"That it is," the old woman said. "But better it would be for me if I had a stout rope to pull my bucket from my well."

Nathan went and got the plough rope to give to her. "I do not take without giving in return," said the old woman, and she handed Nathan a bridle for a horse. Then she said, "Iron is not only used to make a pot."

On that day, Nathan caught three fish. When his mother was cooking the fish for supper, Nathan told her about the old woman.

"She is well known as a spae-wife[2]," said his mother. "You mark well whatever she says to you, and do not forget her words."

---

[2] *Spae-wife* is a Scots language term for a fortune-telling woman.

The days passed, and when the time for spring planting was almost gone, there arrived another night when the moon shone silver. Nathan looked from the window of the croft and saw a dark horse standing by the loch.

"The water kelpie!" he cried out.

His mother tried to distract him, but Nathan was determined. "If we are to live this winter then we must plough the fields straight away. The only way to do it is if I can capture the kelpie and make it work for me."

"What makes you think you can succeed when your father failed?" his mother demanded. "The legend says no man can ride the water kelpie and live!"."

When his mother fell asleep, Nathan put the worn shawl around his shoulders. And, taking the horse bridle, he climbed out the window and went towards the loch. There stood the kelpie, as if it awaited him.

"But you are a bonnie beastie," Nathan murmured. He raised his hand to grasp the horse's mane so that he could haul himself up on its back. Then he paused and remembered the words of the old woman when she gave him his first gift:

"It can be better to sit upon a plaidie than wrap it round you."

So Nathan took the shawl from his shoulders and spread it over the creature's back. Then he grabbed its mane and mounted the kelpie.

For a single second the beast stood still. Then it swelled in size so that Nathan saw his cottage and his mother, a tiny figure at the door, shrieking for him to jump off at once.

"I will not jump off," Nathan called out.

When the kelpie heard this, it snorted and tossed its head. Then it spoke in a husky voice." "No man can ride a kelpie and live. Now you are doomed as your father was before you, for I will not do as you command." Smoke and fire came from its mouth, and it wrenched its head around to face the loch so that it could ride into the water and drown its rider.

Nathan leaned forward and gripped the mane tighter. Beneath his fingers Nathan felt the silky hair change to thick, slimy serpents. Spitting and hissing, the green snakes in the kelpie's mane tried to wind themselves around Nathan's hands, twist their way between his fingers, and coil around his wrists.

And Nathan repeated the words of the woman after the second gift:

"Salt can be used to kill rather than to cure." He quickly slackened the little bag of salt at his waist and crushed the lumps between his palms. At once the snakes shrank and withered, and Nathan could grasp the kelpie's head and pull it the way he wanted it to go.

The kelpie was enraged. It thrashed out with its back legs three times and with its forelegs six times. Then the creature reared and plunged and tried to turn its head away from the land. But Nathan held fast. He kept himself sitting on the old woman's plaid and didn't let his legs touch the back or the sides of the beast so that he wouldn't become stuck.

Nathan recalled the words of the old woman when she gave him the third gift.:

"Iron is not only used to make a pot."

He knew that the metal parts of the bridle were made of iron, so he leaned down and slipped the bridle on. He put the iron bit into the mouth of the kelpie. At once the beast quieted and became tame. It would do whatever Nathan wanted.

Nathan trotted towards his croft and called to his mother to bring out their plough and to run and borrow a rope from their neighbour. Nathan harnessed the kelpie horse to the plough and led it up and down until all the fields were ploughed.

When the fields were done, Nathan waited until the next silver moon. Then he led the kelpie to the water's edge. He slid the bit from its mouth and watched as the creature kicked up its heels and trotted into the water.

And that is the story of the water kelpie of Loch Ness, where the legend was true: no man can master the water kelpie, but a boy did.

Sturdy Tiger was a hard worker but spent holidays and all his free time with his family. He liked to play ball in the courtyard and watched football games on the TV. Daddy Sturdy was also a great painter, and today he was teaching his daughters the colours of the rainbow. In Igbo, of course!

"First of all, the name of the rainbow in Igbo is "egwurukwu". Can you sing with me, Love and Purity?"

"Mme, or obara obara, is red as the heart. Edo is yellow as the sun. Uhie Ocha is pink as the rose Akwukwondu, or ndu-ndu, is green as the grass. Ugo, or Ododo, is purple like a beetroot. Uhie-edo, or Oroma, is orange as the pumpkin. Atulu, or amaloji, is blue as the ocean. Ojii is black as the night. Ocha is white as the snow.

"You now are able to say the Igbo names of the colours!"

It was already four o' clock! It was time for an afternoon snack and a story. While Love and Purity ate in the garden, Sturdy Tiger got ready to tell them a story from IGBOLAND!

Sturdy Tiger threw some pebbles at the picket fence, and magically turned into a snake, who started to hiss the following story.

Many decades ago, Mbeku the tortoise had a magnificent shell. It was so smooth and clear and shiny, it even glowed in the dark. The tortoise Mbeku had also a bottomless hole for a stomach and would stop at nothing to fill it.

One day in the forest, Mbeku found a group of birds celebrating. Curious, he asked what was happening, and they replied that they had received an invitation from the king of Skyland. Mbeku wanted to go with them, but a swallow laughed at him and said he could not come because he could not fly.

Mbeku grinned slyly. He was known as a trickster creature, so he had in mind a plan to persuade the birds to give him some feathers. After some persuasion, the birds decided to each give a feather to him. Mbeku took the feathers to Ngwele, the lizard, and asked her to help him make wings. Ngwele was a wonderful maker of things and Mbeku's only friend. Ngwele toiled all night while Mbeku perfected his plan. The next day, when the tortoise joined the birds, he was wearing a glorious pair of wings and a cunning smile. Mbeku told the birds that the Skylanders love fancy names, so they needed to change theirs. Mbeku announced his name after the birds. "My new name is.." he paused importantly. "Aaaaall-of-you!" The birds burst out laughing.

The king of the Skylanders welcomed the guests with a grand festival. As spokesman, Mbeku introduced the birds by their fancy new names. But to their surprise, he majestically introduced himself as, "Aaaaall-of-you", the king of the earth dwellers."

The Skylanders were very impressed. "How magnificent he is! Long live King Aaaaall-of-you!" The Skylanders served a feast of bountiful heaps of mouth-watering fruits, berries, nuts, and honeycombs.

Mbeku bowed low. "A thousand thanks, noble king. But allow me to ask: For whom have you prepared this royal feast?"

The king spread his arms wide and spoke to the crowd in front of him. "Why, for Aaaaall-of-you, of course!"

Trickster Mbeku turned to the birds. "Skylanders always feed the spokesman first," he hissed. "So don't any of you touch the food. You heard the king name who this meal is for, and you know whose name that is!" And with that, Mbeku dug into the feast.

Surprised, the Skylanders murmured to each other, "It must be the custom of the earth dwellers to let their king eat first."

"Don't worry," Mbeku mumbled to the birds. "Your turn will come." But after Mbeku was finally finished, there wasn't a scrap left for the birds, and it was time to depart. A thick cloud descended as the king led the earth dwellers to an enormous tree at the edge of Skyland. The Skylanders bid their visitors goodbye and then disappeared back into the mist. All at once, the angry birds set upon greedy Mbeku. They ripped off his wings and threw them over the edge of Skyland. "No!" cried Mbeku, as his wings sailed out of sight.

Mbeku put on a great show, until they took pity on the pathetic creature before them. "But what can we do?" asked the swallow. " Your wings are gone."

"Please," begged the cunning Mbeku, "fly down to my friend Ngwele and ask her to build a huge pile of all the softest things she can find in the clearing. Do this for me, and I will never trick you again." The instant the birds left, Mbeku's tears stopped. He grinned, and then he laughed wildly.

Unseen, the little swallow had hung back to hunt down a flea in her feathers. From the shadows, she heard and saw everything. Quick as a wink, she was off and telling the others how, once more, they had been fooled. Greatly annoyed, the birds planned a trick of their own. The birds went to Ngwele. "Mbeku has decided to stay longer in the sky," they said, "but he wanted us to ask you to gather all the hardest things you can find and build a huge pile in the clearing."

"What for?" asked Ngwele.

"He didn't say," replied a hummingbird. Then the birds disappeared deep into the forest to wait until the rains had come and gone.

From Skyland, Mbeku watched a tiny dot below. As Ngwele hurried back and forth, the pile she was building grew. "Good," he muttered. "Now for a nice, soft landing." He took aim and a deep breath. Then he jumped. Down, down he hurtled, the wind whistling in his ears.

He fell and fell and fell. And just when Mbeku began to wonder if he would ever land, he did! The crash thundered through the forest, and his shell scattered in a million pieces.

"Oh, your shell!" cried Ngwele, when she saw what had happened.

Determined to put the shell back together, Ngwele began to collect the pieces. She had just gathered the last, tiniest bits when the rains came splashing down. In the comfort of her shelter, all through the rainy season, Ngwele laboured over the shell while Mbeku looked on.

But when the work was finished, Mbeku was bitterly disappointed. His mended shell was rugged and checked and dull. Instead of thanking the lizard, he complained.

Early one morning, long after the rains had ended, Mbeku dared to take his first walk in the forest. He had not gone a dozen steps when he heard familiar twittering coming his way. "Birds," muttered Mbeku. "The last creatures I want to meet in my hideous shell!" Then Mbeku drew himself into his checked shell and lay as still as a stone. Babbling merrily, the birds landed all around him. A pigeon and the swallow, thinking Mbeku was a rock, perched right on top of him. The birds all laughed to think they had finally outsmarted Mbeku, while the rock started to smile noiselessly.

Love Ladybug often played as an explorer. She loved to spin her globe and decide where she could go that day. She put on her backpack, and walked around the house, discovering with her imagination the world. She also loved animals and she had already decided to become a veterinarian. She loved dogs, and for this reason she dreamed of travelling to Romania, like her mother did seven years ago in order to help all the stray dogs. Love Ladybug liked to tell everybody the following tale. It was written in Romania by her mother with four amazing girls.

Love Ladybug threw some pebbles at the picket fence and she magically turned into a dog, who started to bark the following story.

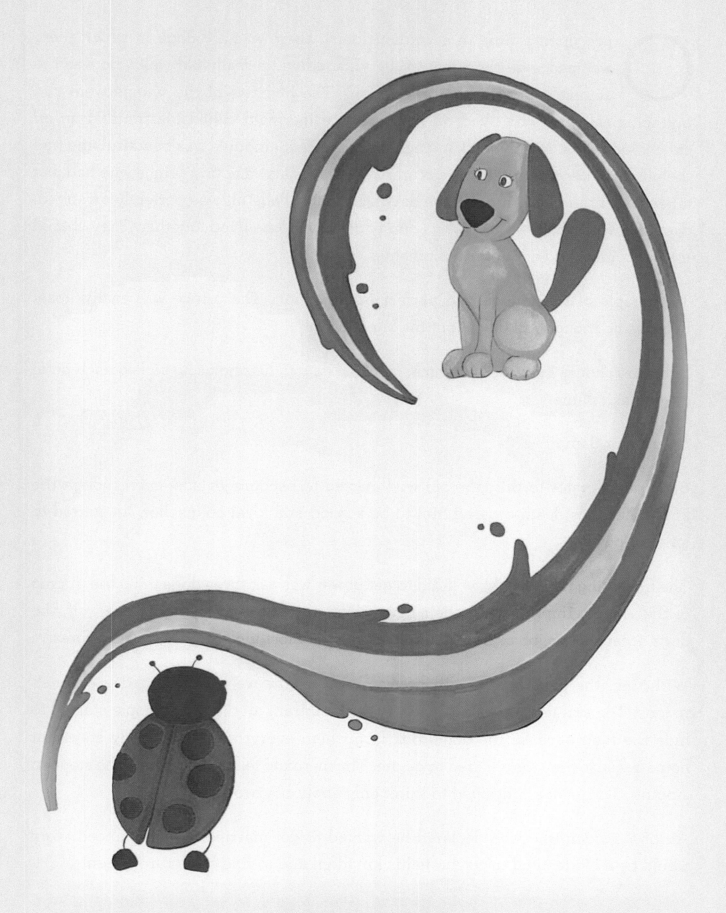

Once upon a time in a verdant forest, there was a village in which there was peace all the time. In the village lived a really old wolf who was the counsellor of the entire kingdom. The beauties of the village were two mythological girls who lived on the border: a mermaid called Marina and an elf called Samodiva. Marina had an enchanting voice. Samodiva was beautiful and had the power to become as tiny as a crumb. There was also a young prince who had just taken the throne after his father's death. In that village all was perfectly arranged, even the weather. Every day was a sunny day. Everyone lived together. They shared meals, homes, and a lot of fun moments.

The people of the village had perfect organisation. The prince was really upset because he thought all day about his big choice:

"Oh, who should I choose? Help me, my little daisy", he said as he picked each petal off for each name.

"Marina or Samodiva?"

Being a spectator to this, the old wolf started to become jealous, even though the king before his death ordered him to be a good and loyal counsellor, he started to long for power.

The first thing that the old wolf did to get power was ask three dogs to be the guards of the village. Impressed by their new power, and showing loyalty to the wolf, the dogs accepted the job and started to become the most violent guards of the forest.

With that, the peace in the village was broken. The weather changed everyone's moods. The sun left the village, and it started to rain all day. The people started to hide the food because the dogs took from them everything. Everybody stayed at home because they were scared to go out. The mermaid felt depressed, so she stopped singing. The prince continued to think only about his two loves.

All of a sudden, the wolf declared he wanted to get married. He announced there would be a big festival to celebrate his kingdom and to find his future queen!

This news scared the prince. He was ashamed about his absence and for the cruelty of this new government. He wallowed in his misery because the kingdom his father created was destroyed.

Meanwhile, the village had never seen a festival like this. Food from the entire world was cooked by the most famous chef in the region. One million exotic flowers decorated the village square.

Music and dances continued all day long. Millions of people from other regions came to participate in this historical event. The entire village was invited to the royal table, even the prince. During the royal meal, seeing an opportunity the prince tried to kill the wolf with poisoned food. But the three dogs, on high-alert, discovered the prince's plan. The prince tried to run away, but the dogs caught him and put him in the prison of the castle.

Samodiva, distressed by the situation of the woebegone prince, used her secret power to help him. She became small, like a butterfly, and passed the dogs without being recognised. She crossed through the bars of his cell and brought him food, company, and a lot of love. The news of the prince's incarceration spread through the village and the inhabitants started to organise a protest in front of the castle.

The mermaid decided to use her magical voice to restore the happiness in the village. With her fabulous singing, she entranced the wolf and the dogs; they started to do everything she wanted. The first thing that the mermaid asked was for the prince. The order was done: the prince was free. He married Samodiva, and they lived together for the village. Then, Marina made the wolf and dogs renounce their power and live in peace with the other citizens. Finally, she asked the sun to come back to light up the rest of their lives in sunshine.

"It is time for bed." Dreamer Panda announced to her daughters and she tucked them under the blankets.

Dreamer Panda then sang the last nursery rhyme of the day with them and they all danced together.

> "The pretty laundress is washing the napkins
> for the poors souls of the city
> Jump!
> Jump again!
> Do a twirl!
> Do a twirl another time.
> Look up!
> Look down!
> Choose someone to kiss!"

Dreamer Panda and Sturdy Tiger started to sing their own goodnight song:

"Good night, ka chi foo, buonanotte, senay leyti, dobranoc, bonne nuit, noapte buna to the apples of my eye."

The day ended as this story. With a kiss.

Bibliography

The stories from Scotland and Africa were excerpted and adapted from the following publications:

1. THE BROWNIE OF FERN GLEN: Grierson, Elizabeth, Scottish Fairy Book, The. Reprint of the J.B. Lippincott Company 1910 Philadelphia edition, Project Gutenberg, 2011. http://www.gutenberg.org/files/37532/37532-h/37532-h.htm# Page 204

2. THE WATER KELPIE: An Illustrated Treasury of Scottish Folk and Fairy Tales, Theresa Breslina and Kate Leiper, Flori Book, Eighth printing 2019.

3. THE FLYING TORTOISE. An Igbo tale. Retold by Tololwa M. Mollel Illustrated by Barbara Spurll, Clarion Books.

4. AULO'. CANTO-POESIA DALL'ERITREA di RIBKA SIBHATU, SINNOS EDITOR.

5. https://www.masteranylanguage.com/c/b/it9ly840sIgL/98-Igbo-Colors-Learn-Step-By-Step

WONDERING WANDERING WRITER

(Alessia Bruni, June 25th, 1987)

In the last ten years, she has conducted research and written her academic thesis on generational relationships, which started with a traineeship with the Italian TV producer "RAI" in her hometown—Torino. She ended up in a European voluntary project in Romania called "Linking Generations": you can find more information about it on her blog "Wondering Wandering Writer". In 2018, there was the birth of her gorgeous daughter, Chikaima Maitea; then in 2020 she doubled her happiness with the birth of Chimamanda Lavinia. Both of them came to the world when God gave her the opportunity to find the love of her life, the one who brought her a rainbow after the rain!

(Rosa Iannello, December 8th, 1991)

Through a fortuitous meeting, Wondering Wandering Writer teamed up with CinnaMom, a highly skilled and talented artist, who was happily shelving her gift in order to be a wise wife and mother. As cinnamon elevates the taste of an ordinary apple pie, the illustrator's skills bring the Chuk family and all the characters in this book to life in an array of beautiful colours.

Printed in the United States
by Baker & Taylor Publisher Services